Little Bear's Christmas

Norbert Landa

Little Bear's Christmas

Illustrated by

Marlis Scharff-Kniemeyer

LITTLE TIGER PRESS

It was autumn in Bear Valley. The wind ripped the bright leaves from the trees and swept them into great rustling heaps.

"I can do something you can't!" shouted Bertie Bear gleefully. He scrambled up a tree and then let himself drop into a soft pile of leaves below.

Wally and Wilma Wolf watched him.

"Autumn leaves are the best!" shouted Bertie.

"I don't *think* so!" snorted Wally. "Winter snow is better."

"Snow? What's that?" asked the little bear.

"You don't know what snow is because you bears sleep through the winter," said Wilma.

"You're just saying that because you're jealous you can't climb trees," growled Bertie.

The next day the three friends went out to fly kites. Bertie's kite flew the highest.

"Flying kites may be fun," said Wally grumpily, "but Christmas is better. Santa Claus brings wonderful presents, and we all sing Christmas carols."

"I've never heard of Santa Claus," laughed Bertie. "But if you wolves sing the way you howl, I'd rather be asleep!"

The following morning Bertie, Wally, and Wilma went to gather mushrooms.

"Here's another one!" called Bertie. "Look how many mushrooms I've found already. We'll have a delicious supper tonight."

Wally and Wilma looked glumly into their empty baskets.

"Mushrooms are yummy!" said Wilma.

"Maybe, but honey cakes and chocolate hearts from Santa Claus are best," said Wally.

That evening, Bertie asked his mother to tell him all about winter, the snow, and Santa Claus.

"Winter is very cold and bleak," said Mrs. Bear. "The mushrooms and berries disappear, and even the rain freezes. It turns white and settles on the ground, and everyone calls it snow. Sensible people, like us bears, go to bed and stay there until the warm spring arrives."

"And what about Santa Claus?" asked Bertie.

"I was coming to him," said Mrs. Bear. "People who don't sleep through the winter aren't as lucky as we are. They have to trudge about in the cold snow. Santa Claus brings them presents to give them something to look forward to in the dark days of winter."

"What does he look like?"

"Well, I've never seen him, but they say he wears a red coat and has a white beard."

Mrs. Bear gave Bertie a big hug and sang him a lullaby.

"I suppose we bears *do* have to sleep through Christmas," said Bertie to himself, "but I still want to see Santa Claus. And I think I know how to do it. If I sleep as much as I can now, I'll be wide awake for Christmas."

The next day, Bear Valley was shrouded in fog. Then it started to rain. Wally and Wilma sailed their boats in the puddles, but Bertie stayed in bed.

"What's the matter?" asked Mrs. Bear. "Aren't you feeling well?"

"No, I'm fine," said Bertie. "I just want to sleep a little longer."

"Sleep? At this time of day?" Mrs. Bear was worried and called Dr. Wolf.

Dr. Wolf checked Bertie's tongue and took his temperature. "This little one's fine," he said. "Maybe the weather is making him tired. I can feel snow coming. But I'm sure he'll be bright as a button by Christmas."

Christmas? Bertie listened hard.

"*Shh*, doctor! Please don't mention Christmas!" whispered Mrs. Bear. "You know we bears sleep through the winter."

"Yes, yes, I forgot," he said. "Well, sleep soundly."

Dr. Wolf hurried home. It was growing very cold, and dark clouds hung over Bear Valley. Snow was on its way.

A few days later Mrs. Bear prepared the cottage for their winter sleep. She tidied the kitchen, swept the floors, and hung a sack of grain from the ceiling to keep it safe from the greedy mice. Then she locked the door, closed the shutters, and yawned.

"Time for bed," she said, giving Bertie a good-night kiss. "Sleep well, little cub, until springtime." Mrs. Bear went into her bedroom, but came out again almost immediately. "Have you seen my alarm clock?" she asked. Bertie closed his eyes and lay as still as he could.

"Goodness, he's fast asleep already!" said Mrs. Bear. "Never mind. I don't need an alarm clock. The spring sunshine will wake me up." She tiptoed out of the room.

Bertie laughed quietly to himself. "I've hidden the alarm clock under my bed! It'll wake me up at Christmas—and then . . ." But Bertie fell asleep before he could finish.

In the valley the snow began to fall in thick, white flakes. All was quiet and still. It was very peaceful. Inside the cottage the little bear slept for a very long time.

Suddenly the alarm clock went off. Bertie nearly fell out of bed in surprise. What a noise! He turned it off as soon as he could. Did Mrs. Bear hear it, too? No, all Bertie could hear was his mother's gentle snoring. He threw open the shutters and looked out.

It was a miracle! Someone had covered the whole valley
with a white, fluffy blanket, as thick and soft as a featherbed.
So *this* was snow! And, thought Bertie, where there's snow,
Santa Claus can't be far away.

Bertie tied on his scarf, opened the door, and stepped out into
the shining white snow. He listened carefully but couldn't hear a
sound.

"I'm going to find Santa Claus!" he whispered to himself as
he plodded up the hill. Every step left a small, deep paw print.
The snow felt fluffy, but it wasn't as warm as a featherbed.
In fact, it was very cold. Amazing!

At last Bertie reached the top of the hill. From here he could see across the whole valley. He looked in every direction. Where was Santa Claus?

Then he felt something cold and wet on his nose. A snowflake! And another! And another one again! Snowflakes came dancing down from the sky, and Bertie danced with them until he was dizzy. By the time he stopped for breath there were so many whirling snowflakes that he could hardly see past his nose.

"Santa Claus, where are you?" he shouted. "Can you hear me?"

But Santa Claus didn't answer.

Everything was silent.

The snow continued to flutter down from the sky. Bertie waited. His feet were getting cold. Then he began to feel hungry. And soon he started to feel frightened. Darkness was falling.

"How can I find Santa Claus in the dark?" he sighed. "I'd better go home while I can still find my way."

Bertie slid down the hill, following the paw prints he had made before. But the snow fell quickly, and soon his paw prints were covered over. Now Bertie didn't know where he was, or how to find his way home.

"Help!" he shouted. "I'm lost and I want to go home!"

Bertie listened hard for an answer.
He couldn't hear anything except a distant
howling. Could that be Wally and Wilma
singing? No, it was only the wind. But then
Bertie heard a faint jingling. Then a sleigh
appeared through the snowflakes.

"Hey! Stop!" shouted the little bear.
"Please wait for me!"

The driver pulled on his reins and turned
around. He was wrapped from head to toe in
a thick blanket, and all Bertie could see was
a friendly face with twinkling blue eyes.
The little bear stepped nearer and stared,
astonished. The sleigh had no wheels!
It sped across the snow on huge skis, pulled
by reindeer with magnificent antlers.

"Hello, Bertie!" cried the driver.
"Where have you come from? Shouldn't
all little bears be asleep by now?"

"Well, yes, they should, really,"
murmured Bertie, embarrassed. "But I
wanted to look for Santa Claus, and now
I can't find my way home!"

"I thought so," laughed the driver.
"Come with me—and hold tight!"

Bertie climbed aboard, amazed. "Giddyup!" shouted
the driver, and the reindeer gave a mighty leap. In no time
the sleigh was flying through the air. Bertie was terrified.
The ground seemed so far below them. "Hey! Where are
we going?" he called out nervously.

"We're taking you home, of course!"

In no time at all the sleigh swept back to earth and
landed right in front of the bears' cottage.

The driver leaped down from his seat and threw off the
blanket. Now Bertie could see that he was wearing a red coat!

"Y-y-you're Santa Claus . . ." stammered the little bear.

"Of course I am," laughed Santa. "But quiet now or you'll
wake up your mother." He pulled a cloth off the sleigh, and
Bertie saw a huge heap of packages and parcels and presents.

"Now, what would you like for Christmas?" asked
Santa Claus.

Bertie thought hard. "I'll have—honey cakes and
chocolate hearts, please. And for Mommy . . . chocolate
hearts and honey cakes!"

"That's easy," said Santa Claus. He rummaged about
in the sleigh and finally pulled out two packages.
Together they carried them to the cottage.

"I have to go now,"
whispered Santa Claus. "Wally
and Wilma are waiting for me.
But I'll tell you what. Next Christmas
I'll bring you presents, too—but only if you're
asleep. Is that a deal?"
"It's a deal," said Bertie.

Bertie watched as Santa Claus scrambled back up into his sleigh. It shot off so fast it sent sparks flying. Soon he could only see a tiny speck in the dark sky. Or was that a star? Bertie was much too tired to think about it now. He tiptoed into his room, hid the presents in his toy chest, and crawled into bed. Then he fell asleep.

When Bertie woke up again it was daylight. He could smell flowers. Birds were twittering. Mrs. Bear had thrown open the windows.

"Good morning, little one!" she cried, kissing Bertie on the nose. "Time to get up! It's springtime!"

Springtime? Bertie rubbed his eyes and yawned. Then he remembered. "Santa Claus was here!"

"The mice were here, you mean," called Mrs. Bear from the kitchen. "Look what they've done to our sack of grain. They've chewed through the ropes and have eaten every scrap! What will we have for breakfast?"

"Honey cakes and chocolate hearts!" shouted Bertie, running to his toy box. "And chocolate hearts and honey cakes!" Then he told Mrs. Bear the whole story.

"And the best thing is—Santa Claus will come again next year!" said the little bear.

"Yes," agreed Mrs. Bear, "but only if you're asleep!"

A little later Wally and Wilma peeped through the window. They sniffed the air curiously. "That's funny!" they said. "Your house smells like Christmas!"

Mrs. Bear and Bertie winked at one another. "We bears always celebrate Christmas a little late," they said. "Didn't you know that?"

LITTLE TIGER PRESS
N16 W23390 Stoneridge Drive, Waukesha, WI 53188
First published in the United States 1999
Originally published in Germany 1997 by
Ravensburger Buchverlag under the title Wo bist du, Weihnachtsmann?
Copyright © Ravensburger Buchverlag 1997
Illlustration: Marlis Scharff-Kniemeyer · Text: Norbert Landa
English translation by Anna Trenter
All rights reserved

Library of Congress Cataloging-in-Publication Data
Landa, Norbert. [Wo bist du, Weihnachtsmann? English]
Little Bear's Christmas / Norbert Landa ;
illustrated by Marlis Scharff-Kniemeyer ;
[English translation by Anna Trenter].—1st American ed. p.   cm.
Summary : Determined to find out what Santa Claus looks like, a little bear
sleeps as much as he can before winter hibernation, wakes himself up with his
mother's alarm clock, and sets out into the snowy countryside.
ISBN 1-888444-60-6 (hc)
[1. Bears Fiction. 2. Santa Claus Fiction. 3. Snow Fiction. 4. Christmas Fiction.]
I. Scharff-Kniemeyer, Marlis, ill. II. Trenter, Anna. III. Title
PZ7.L23165Li 1999 [E]—dc21 99-25069 CIP
Printed in Germany · First American Edition
1 3 5 7 9 10 8 6 4 2